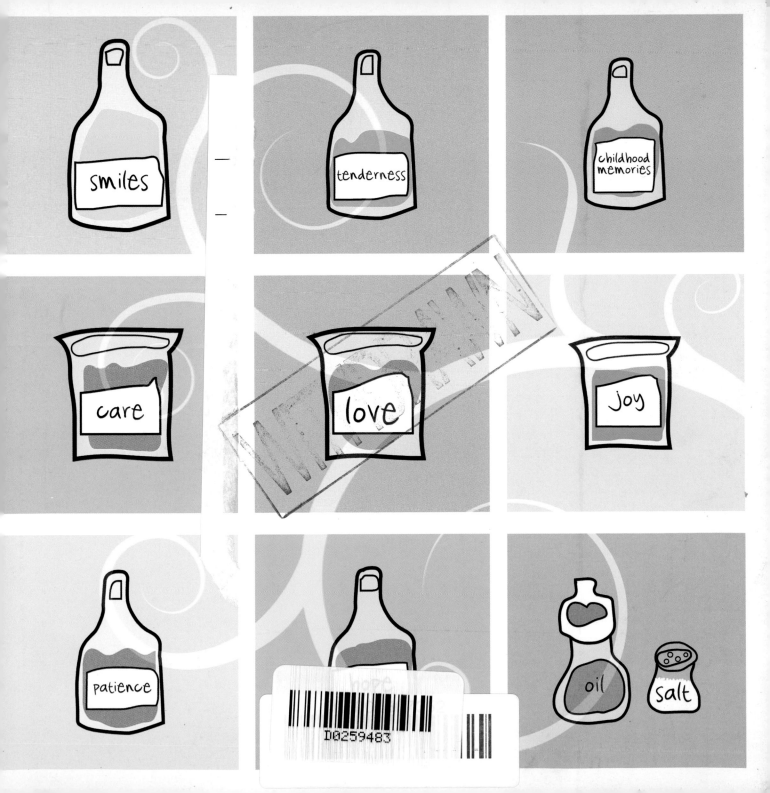

You, me and the breast

First published in Great Britain by Pinter & Martin Ltd 2011

Text copyright © 2011 Mònica Calaf
Illustrations copyright © 2011 Mikel Fuentes

ISBN 978-1-905177-52-3

British Library Cataloguing-in-Publication Data
A catalogue record for this book is available from the British Library

Printed by Tien Wah Press Ltd, Singapore

Pinter & Martin Ltd
6 Effra Parade
London SW2 1PS

www.pinterandmartin.com

You, me and the breast

Text Mònica Calaf

Illustrations Mikel Fuentes

pinter & martin

When you came
out of my tummy...

...the first thing you looked for
was my breast.

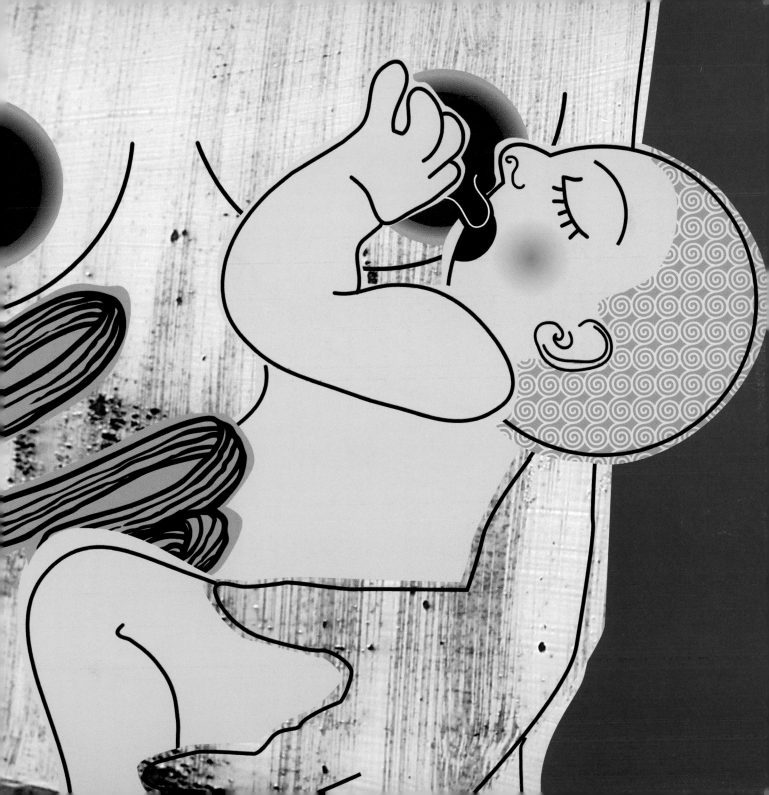

My nipple darkened so you could see
it better and gave off a rich smell,
so that you could find it with your
tiny nose.

At night we would sleep cuddled up
next to each other, close to daddy.

During the day we would
go everywhere together.

We would meet other mummies with their new baby boys and girls.

When you were hungry
I had your food ready.

Even when we were at the beach,
or in the swimming pool!

Often I was breastfeeding you while doing something else at the same time: stirring the saucepan...

Bla Bla Bla Bla Bla Bla

talking on the phone...
going shopping...

reading a magazine, doing
exercise to get back into shape...

watering the garden...

eating...

When you were breastfeeding,
you were relaxed, happy and contented.
We both loved these intimate
and special moments.

Often you fell asleep after breastfeeding and I took the opportunity to do my own thing...

When your teeth came through, I helped you learn to suck without biting.

Little by little you started to learn
to drink from a cup and to eat with
a spoon, but you still needed milk
from my breast.

Suckling also helped me to comfort you. If you fell over, felt scared or unwell you enjoyed a cuddle at the breast to make you feel better.

As you started to grow, you began
to eat the same food as mummy
and daddy.

As you got older you would ask me to tell you a story at bedtime, and from then on you have not needed to suckle any more to fall asleep.

I hope you liked our story
You, me and the breast!
Good night!

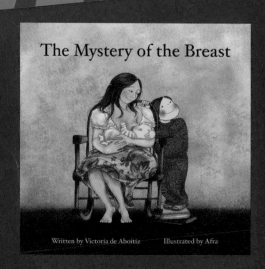
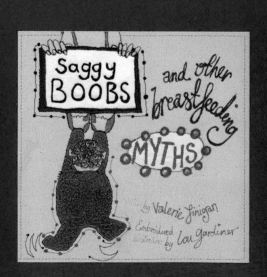